T A L E S   O F

Rudyard Kipling

R E T O L D   T I M E L E S S   C L A S S I C S

Perfection Learning®

Retold by L. L. Owens

Editor: Paula J. Reece
Illustrator: Greg Hargreaves

For information, contact
Perfection Learning® Corporation,
1000 North Second Avenue, P.O. Box 500
Logan, Iowa 51546-0500.
Phone: 1-800-831-4190 • Fax: 1-712-644-2392

Paperback ISBN 0-7891-5069-7
Cover Craft® ISBN 0-7807-9037-5
Printed in the U.S.A.

Table of Contents

Rudyard Kipling
(1865–1936)

Rudyard Kipling was a novelist, short story writer, and poet. In 1907 he received the Nobel Prize for Literature. Both children and adults love his work.

Joseph Rudyard Kipling was born in Bombay, India, in 1865. Kipling was named after his grandfather, Joseph, and after the lake in England where his parents first met. His parents were British citizens. His father was a soldier and an artist. Kipling spent his early life in India. The family's Hindu servants taught him the Hindustani language. They told him Indian folktales that he remembered all his life.

When Kipling was six years old, his parents sent him to school in England. Kipling lived with his Aunt Rosa, who was cruel and often beat him. Kipling later went to the United Services College, a boarding school for children of British soldiers. There the older boys bullied him, and the teachers whipped him. Kipling never forgot his miserable childhood. He wrote about these experiences in many of his stories.

Kipling left school at the age of 17. His parents offered to send him to the university, but he refused. He wanted to go back to India, get a job, and recapture the happiness of his earlier life. He joined the staff of the *Civil and Military Gazette* in Lahore. This paper was written for British colonists, not for the Indian people. In addition to his job, Kipling began to write short stories and poems. Many of these were printed in the *Gazette*. In 1889 Kipling traveled to England to write a series of articles for the *Gazette*. The *London Times* wrote a favorable review of his work. This recognition helped Kipling's writing career.

In 1890 Kipling moved to the United States. He wrote a novel, *The Naulakha,* with his friend, Wolcott Balestier. The novel never became popular, but while working on it, Kipling met Balestier's sister, Caroline. They were married in 1892.

In 1896 Kipling and his wife moved back to England. By this time his work was attracting notice. He wrote a book of poems about English soldiers in India. One of these poems, "Gunga Din," became so famous that it was made into a movie many years later.

Kipling also wrote novels and short stories as well as books for children. In 1894 he wrote *The Jungle Book*. This collection of stories became Kipling's most famous work. Children all over the world love the tales of tigers; elephants; and Mowgli, the boy raised by wolves. These stories were so popular that Kipling later wrote *The Second Jungle Book* and *Just So Stories.*

In his later years, Kipling became less popular. He strongly believed in colonialism, Britain's right to conquer and rule other countries. Most of his later works were essays that supported his views. These views offended many people.

Kipling died in 1936. He is buried in Westminster Abbey, next to the tomb of Charles Dickens. Today most people don't care about his political ideas. They remember only his wonderful stories and poems.

toomai of the Elephants

KALA NAG, WHICH means *Black Snake,* was a great elephant. And a very old one. He had served the country of India for almost 50 years. He had carried guns, tents, and timber. And he had been trained to work with wild elephants.

the fourth generation

Kala Nag's driver was Big Toomai. He was the son of Black Toomai and the grandson of Toomai of the Elephants. All of them had been Kala Nag's drivers. "He has seen three generations of us," said Big Toomai. "He will live to see four. And he fears nothing except me."

"He is afraid of me too," said Little Toomai. He was ten years old and the son of Big Toomai. When Little Toomai was grown, he would take his father's place. Like his father, grandfather, and great-grandfather, he would be an elephant driver.

"Someday you will be old, Kala Nag," Little Toomai said. "Then you will walk in parades. You will wear gold on your back and your ears. And I will ride on your back. That will be good, Kala Nag. But not as good as hunting in the jungle."

"Hunting!" said his father. "You don't know what you are talking about. Forget the jungle! Give me a place with real roads. With stalls and stumps to tie the beasts to. None of this running up and down the hills looking for wild elephants."

Little Toomai didn't say anything. He liked the camp life. He liked to go up paths that only elephants could take. Seeing wild elephants in the distance. The beautiful misty mornings. The careful tracking of the wild elephants. The mad rush of driving them into a stockade.

Little Toomai was as useful as three boys. He would wave his torch to help drive the elephants. But what he liked best was when the elephants filled the stockade. He would climb to the top of one of the posts. He would yell, "Go, Kala Nag! Careful now, Kala Nag. Watch that post!" Kala Nag would fight with the wild elephants that tried to get away. And he would listen to Little Toomai.

But Little Toomai did more than yell. One night he saw that the end of a rope had fallen to the ground. He slid off his post and ran between two elephants. He grabbed the rope and handed it back to a driver.

Kala Nag saw him. The great elephant picked up Little Toomai and handed him to Big Toomai. Little Toomai's father put his son back on the post.

the elephant hunter

The next day Big Toomai scolded Little Toomai. "Why are you catching elephants? Now those foolish hunters have told Petersen Sahib what you did."

Little Toomai was afraid when he heard this. He knew that Petersen Sahib was very powerful. He was in charge of catching elephants for the whole country of India. He knew more about elephants than anyone else.

"What will happen now?" asked Little Toomai.

"Happen!" cried his father. "The worst that can happen! Petersen Sahib is a madman. Why else would he hunt these wild devils? He may expect you to be an elephant catcher now. It is well that this trip is nearly over. Next week we will be done. We will leave this place. And we can forget all this hunting."

Big Toomai went on talking. "I am not a hunter. No one in the family of Toomai of the Elephants is a hunter. Worthless son! Go and take care of Kala Nag. And pray that Petersen Sahib forgets what you did. Or he may make you a wild elephant hunter. Go!"

Little Toomai went off without a word. He checked on Kala Nag. At the same time he told the elephant what had happened.

"No matter," Little Toomai said. "Petersen Sahib has already heard my name. And maybe . . ."

The next few days were busy. Blankets and ropes had to be counted. Each wild elephant had to be walked up and down between two tame elephants. This kept them from causing trouble.

Then Petersen Sahib rode into camp on his elephant, Pudmini. He came to pay the workers, for the hunting season was almost over.

Big Toomai went to get his pay. Little Toomai was right behind him. The head tracker whispered to a friend of his. "There goes one good elephant catcher. Too bad he has to go off with the drivers."

Petersen Sahib turned and said, "What is that you say? I didn't know any of the drivers could rope even a dead elephant."

The head tracker pointed to Little Toomai. Petersen Sahib looked his way, and Little Toomai bowed low.

"He threw a rope?" asked Petersen Sahib. "He is smaller than a pin. Little one, what is your name?"

Little Toomai was afraid to say anything. But Kala Nag was behind him. Little Toomai made a sign with his hand. The elephant caught the boy up in his trunk. He held him level with Petersen Sahib, who still sat on his elephant.

Little Toomai covered his face with his hands. After all, he was only a child. And except with the elephants, he was very shy.

"So," said Petersen Sahib. "Why did you teach your elephant that trick? Was it so you could steal corn from the roofs of houses?"

"Not corn, Sahib," said Little Toomai. "Melons."

All the men started to laugh. Most of them had taught their elephants the same trick when they were boys.

"He is Little Toomai, my son," said Big Toomai. "And he is a very bad boy, Sahib."

"I don't think so," said Petersen Sahib. "Not when he is brave enough to enter a stockade full of wild elephants. Here, little boy. Take these coins and buy some sweets. In time you may be a great elephant hunter."

Petersen Sahib went on. "Just remember, the stockade is no place for children to play."

"Must I stay out of there forever?" asked Little Toomai.

Petersen Sahib smiled. "You must stay out until you see the elephants dance. Come to me when you have seen them. Then I will let you go into the stockade."

Everyone laughed because this was a joke with elephant catchers. It really meant "never." There were great flat clearings in the jungle. They were called "the elephants' ballrooms." But no one had ever seen the elephants dance.

restless elephants

Kala Nag put Little Toomai down. The boy bowed and went away with his father. Soon the drivers and their families set off with the new elephants.

As they marched along, Little Toomai thought of all that had happened. "What did Petersen Sahib mean by 'the elephant dance'?" he asked his mother.

Big Toomai heard him. "That you must never be an elephant catcher. That is what he meant."

Then a driver ahead of them turned around. "Can you bring Kala Nag here, Little

Toomai? I need him to get this wild elephant back into line. I think he smells other elephants in the jungle."

Little Toomai did as he had been asked. But he told the other driver, "There are no elephants in this part of the jungle. We have them all."

"Ho! You think so?" asked the driver. "Everyone knows the elephant hunts are over for the season. And tonight the wild elephants will . . ."

He shook his head and stopped. So Little Toomai asked, "What will they do?"

"Ah, little one," said the driver. "They will dance. Your father would be wise to use heavy chains on his elephants tonight."

"What talk is this?" asked Big Toomai. "My family has worked with elephants for years. We have never heard such foolishness about dances."

"Well, leave your elephants unchained tonight. Then you will see," the driver said.

They kept arguing as they drove the elephants forward. At last they made it to the spot where they would camp for the night.

All the elephants were chained to thick stumps. Extra ropes were tied to the wild elephants. After the elephants were fed, the drivers left for the night.

As the stars came out, Little Toomai sat in front of Kala Nag. The wild elephants pulled at their ropes. Little Toomai could hear them squealing and trumpeting. He could hear voices in the camp. At last he felt sleepy. He lay down on the straw near Kala Nag.

All the elephants began to lie down as well. Soon only Kala Nag was still on his feet. He rocked slowly from side to side. His big ears moved as he listened to the night noises.

Little Toomai slept for some time. When he woke up, the moon was bright. Kala Nag was still standing and listening. In the distance, Little Toomai heard the "hoot-hoot" of a wild elephant.

At that, the elephants all got to their feet. Their grunts woke the drivers. The men came and checked the ropes and chains. One elephant had pulled up the stake that held his chain. So Big Toomai took off Kala Nag's chain. He used it to tie up the new elephant. And he slipped a loop of grass around Kala Nag's leg. Just to remind the elephant that he was tied.

Big Toomai said to Little Toomai, "Take care of Kala Nag if he gets restless." Then he went back to the hut to sleep.

Little Toomai was soon almost asleep again. Then he heard a *snap* as the grass loop broke.

Kala Nag started to move as slowly as a cloud rolling out of a valley. Little Toomai jumped up and ran after him. "Kala Nag!" he cried. "Take me with you!"

The elephant turned and put down his trunk. He lifted Little Toomai onto his back. Then he slipped into the forest.

There was the sound of elephants trumpeting. Then there was silence. Kala Nag moved through the jungle. Little Toomai knew they were going uphill. But he couldn't tell where they were.

Kala Nag stopped at the top of the hill. Below them Little Toomai could see miles and miles of treetops. They were speckled and furry in the moonlight.

The trees closed in over their heads as Kala Nag began moving again. Now he rushed down the steep bank. Little Toomai bent close to the elephant's neck to keep from being knocked to the ground.

There was a splash and the sound of running water. Kala Nag waded across a river. Over the sound of the water, Little Toomai heard other elephants. The mist around him was full of rolling, wavy shadows.

Then they began to climb again. But now they were on a newly made path. It was six feet wide. The jungle grass was bent down low.

Many elephants must have passed by only moments earlier.

the elephants' ballroom

At last Kala Nag stopped. He stood at the edge of a circle of trees. In the middle was a huge open space. The ground had been trampled down as hard as brick. Not a single blade of grass grew in the ring.

In the moonlight, Toomai could see the inky black shadows of elephants. More and more of them came into the circle. Outside the clearing, Toomai could hear the crashing of other elephants. Soon the circle was full.

There were white-tusked males and fat she-elephants. There were little pink calves. There were young elephants whose tusks were just beginning to show. And there were scarred, old bull elephants. Little Toomai even saw Petersen Sahib's elephant, Pudmini. A broken chain dragged from her foot.

Little Toomai knew he was safe as long as he lay still. For even a wild elephant won't drag a man from a tame elephant's neck. A cloud came over the moon. And he sat in the darkness. Once a trunk came up and touched his knee.

Then an elephant trumpeted. The others answered him. And a dull booming noise began.

Little Toomai couldn't tell what the noise was. It grew and grew. Until at last Kala Nag lifted one front leg. Then the other. *One-two. One-two.*

Soon all the elephants were stamping together. It sounded like a war drum beating at the mouth of a cave. The dew fell from the trees until there was no more left to fall. The ground rocked and shook. Little Toomai put his hands over his ears. But still the sound ran through him.

Once or twice he felt Kala Nag move forward. Then the boom of feet on the ground would start up again. It went on and on for hours.

At last morning broke in one sheet of pale yellow. The booming stopped. And before Toomai could move, the elephants were gone. The only ones left were Kala Nag and Pudmini.

Little Toomai looked around the clearing. It was even bigger than it had been the night before. The bushes and grass at the edges had been trampled by the elephants.

Little Toomai's eyes were heavy. "Kala Nag, take me to the camp," he said. "Or I will drop from your neck."

little toomai, the hero

Two hours later they reached camp. The chained elephants began to trumpet. Petersen Sahib looked up from his breakfast as Pudmini and Kala Nag came near.

Little Toomai's face was gray. His hair was wet and full of leaves. He looked down at Petersen Sahib and cried, "The dance! The elephant dance! I have seen it. And now, I die!" Then he slid from Kala Nag's neck.

But two hours later he was fine. The old hunters of the jungle sat in front of him. They gazed at Little Toomai as if he were a spirit. They listened as he told his tale. He ended by saying, "If you don't believe me, send someone to see. They will find that the elephant folk have been dancing."

Little Toomai slept all through the afternoon and evening. While he rested, Petersen Sahib and his men followed the elephants' tracks. They found the clearing where the elephants had danced.

"The boy speaks the truth," said one of the men. "All of this was done last night."

The men looked at one another and wondered. For the ways of elephants are beyond the minds of men.

When they got back to camp, there was a great feast. And Little Toomai was the hero of it all.

At last the flames of the campfire died down. Then the head of all the drivers jumped to his feet. He lifted Little Toomai high into the air. He shouted, "Listen, my brothers! Listen, my lords, the elephants! This little one will no longer be called 'Little Toomai.' He will be called 'Toomai of the Elephants.' Just as his great-grandfather was before him. He has seen what no man has seen before. He will be a great tracker. He will never be harmed in the stockade. Even the charging bull elephant will not crush him."

Then the head driver turned to the elephants. "Give him honor, my lords! He has seen your dance! To Toomai of the Elephants!"

The whole line of elephants raised their trunks. They began to trumpet loudly.

And it was all for Little Toomai. The boy who had seen what no man had seen before. The dance of the elephants!

The White Seal

EVERY SPRING THE seals leave the sea and go to the Northeast Point. A place far away in the Bering Sea. The older males fight with one another for good spots to set up housekeeping. The young males go off to play on the sand dunes.

And so one year a huge gray seal named Sea Catch fought and won his usual spot. His soft, gentle-eyed wife, Matkah, came to meet him. Soon there were millions of seals on the beach. You could hear them for miles. They covered every foot of ground as far as the eye could see.

The First of Its Kind

Matkah's baby was born in the middle of this. Kotick was all head and shoulders. His eyes were the pale blue of water. This was just as tiny seals should be. But something about his coat made his mother look at him closely.

"Sea Catch," she said. "Our baby is going to be white!"

"Empty clam shells and dry seaweed!" cried Sea Catch. "A white seal? There has never been such a thing before!"

"I can't help that," said Matkah. "There's going to be one now." And then she sang the song all seal mothers sing to their babies.

Kotick stayed close to his mother. He paddled along at her side. He learned to get out of the way when his father was fighting with another seal. He ate everything his mother brought to him. And he grew bigger every day.

Now little seals are like children. They can't swim when they are born. So at first Kotick was happy to lie in a pool by the shore. He would paddle when the waves covered him. But he kept an eye out for big waves that might hurt. It took two weeks for him to learn to use his flippers. But after that he knew he belonged in the water.

Kotick had lots of company there. There were thousands of babies his age. All the little seals ducked under the waves. They played on the weedy rocks. They stood on their tails and scratched their heads. And when they spotted a Killer Whale, they got out of the way.

In the fall the seal families began to head for the deep sea. The young males left the sand dunes and played wherever they wanted. Matkah told Kotick, "Next year you will be one of them. But this year you must come with me and learn to catch fish."

They set out together into the deep sea. Matkah showed Kotick how to sleep on his back. No cradle is as gentle as the rocking waves of the ocean.

One day Kotick felt his skin tingle all over. His mother told him that meant bad weather was coming. He must swim away from it.

"Someday you will know where to go," she said. "But for now just follow the wise porpoise." So that is what Kotick did.

"How do you know where to go?" Kotick asked the leader of the porpoises.

The porpoise rolled his eyes and ducked under the water. "My tail tingles," he said. "That means there's a wind behind me."

So Kotick was always learning. Matkah taught him how to follow the fish. She taught him how to dance on top of the waves. She showed him how to jump out of the water like a dolphin. At the end of six months, Kotick knew all he needed to about fishing. And in all that time he never put a flipper on dry land.

Seal Skinners

But then spring came. Kotick lay half asleep in the warm water somewhere to the south. He thought about the beaches of Northeast Point, a thousand miles away. He remembered the games he and his friends had played. He remembered the smell of the seaweed. The roar of the fighting seals.

So he turned north. He swam and swam. Along the way, he met his mates. They were all headed for the same place. Some said, "Greetings, Kotick! This year we are young seals. We can dance in the waves and play on the grass. But where did you get that coat?"

Kotick was almost pure white now. He was very proud of his coat. But he only said, "Swim quickly! We must get back."

And so they all came to the beaches where they had been born. They heard the old seals, their fathers, fighting.

Kotick and his mates went inland. They rolled in the grass. They told stories of what they had done in the sea. They played in the sand dunes.

Then some black-haired men came from behind a hill. Kotick had never seen a man before. So he watched carefully. The other young seals just sat and stared stupidly.

The men were from a village on the island. One was the chief of the seal hunters. Another was Patalamon, his son. They were there to drive some seals to the killing pens.

"Ho!" said Patalamon. "Look! There's a white seal!"

The chief turned pale. "Don't touch him," he said. "There has never been a white seal since I was born. Maybe it is the ghost of a dead seal hunter."

"That seal is unlucky," said Patalamon. "I won't touch him."

"Don't even look at him," said his father. "Just drive off that bunch of young seals. We will skin them today."

So Patalamon rattled some bones in front of a herd of seals. Then he herded them inland. Thousands of seals watched as the others were led off. Still they went on playing.

Kotick was the only one who asked questions. And no one could give him any answers. They just said that the men always led seals off like that.

"I am going to follow," said Kotick.

"The white seal is coming after us," cried Patalamon. "No seal has ever come to the killing grounds alone before!"

"Shh!" said his father. "Don't look at him. That seal is a ghost!"

It took an hour to get to the killing grounds. At last the men stopped, and so did the seals. Then 10 or 12 more men came. Each had a heavy club in his hands. The chief said, "Let's go!" And the men began to hit the seals on the head.

Ten minutes later all of Kotick's friends were dead. That was enough for Kotick. He turned and hurried back to the sea. He reached the spot where the sea lions sit on the edge of the surf. He threw himself into the water and rocked there.

"What's the matter?" asked one sea lion.

"They're killing all the young seals!" cried Kotick.

"Don't be silly," said the sea lion. "Your friends are as noisy as ever. They can't all be dead. The seal hunters only kill some of the seals. They have been doing it for 30 years."

"It's awful," said Kotick.

"I suppose it is, from your point of view," said the sea lion. "But you seals come back here every year. And the men know it. So it will happen again and again. Unless you find an island where no men ever go."

"Is there an island like that?" asked Kotick.

"I haven't found one. But go to Walrus Island. Talk to Sea Vitch. He may know something," said the sea lion.

So Kotick swam to Walrus Island. He landed close to old Sea Vitch. The walrus was big, ugly, fat-necked, and long-tusked. He had no manners at all—except when he was asleep. Which he was now.

"Wake up!" barked Kotick.

"Hah! Ho! What's that?" asked Sea Vitch. He hit the walrus next to him. That walrus hit the next one. And so on until all the walrus were awake.

"It's me," said Kotick. He bobbed in the water.

"Well! May I be skinned!" said Sea Vitch.

Kotick didn't want to hear any more about skinning. He had seen enough of it. So he asked, "Is there a place where seals can be safe? A place where men never go?"

"Find out for yourself," said Sea Vitch. "We're busy here."

Kotick jumped in the air. He shouted, "Clam eater! Clam eater!"

This was a rude thing to say. Sea Vitch acted

very tough. But he had never caught so much as a fish in his whole life.

Soon all the gulls and puffins took up the cry. They all called, "Clam eater! Clam eater!" Now Sea Vitch was very angry.

"Now will you tell me?" asked Kotick.

"Go and ask the Sea Cows," said Sea Vitch.

"How will I know them when I meet them?" asked Kotick.

A gull screamed out the answer. "They are the only things in the sea uglier than Sea Vitch! Uglier, and with even worse manners!"

Kotick swam back to Northeast Point. There he found that no one cared about what he was doing. They told him that men had always herded off young seals.

"This is what you must do," said Kotick's father. "Grow up and be a big seal like me. Then the men will leave you alone."

Even Matkah, his mother, was little help. "You will never be able to stop the killing," she said. "Go and play in the sea, Kotick."

The Search for the Sea Cows

Kotick went off with a very heavy heart. And that fall he left the beach as soon as he could.

He had an idea. He was going to find the Sea Cows. He was going to find a quiet island where the seals could live. Somewhere men could not get them.

So Kotick explored by himself. He met with more adventures than can be told. He had many narrow escapes. But he never met a Sea Cow.

For five years Kotick searched for a safe island. Every spring he came back to Northeast Point. And every fall he set off to search again.

One spring Kotick headed for Northeast Point as usual. On the way he stopped on an island full of green trees. He found an old, old seal who was dying. Kotick caught fish for the old seal. And he told him about his search.

"Now I am going back," said Kotick. "And if I am herded to the killing grounds, I don't care."

The old seal said, "Try one more time. I am the last of my herd. Men killed us by the thousands. But I heard a story once. It said that a white seal would come out of the North. He would lead the seal people to a quiet place. I am old, and I won't live to see that day. But others will. Try one more time."

Kotick said, "I am the only white seal. And I am the only seal who ever thought of looking for new islands."

He headed back to Northeast Point again. There his mother begged him to marry and settle down. For he was full-grown and as big and strong as his father.

"Give me one more year," said Kotick.

Another seal thought she would wait to marry too. On the night before he set off again, Kotick danced on the waves with her. Then he went west, following the trail of a school of fish.

Kotick chased the fish until he was tired. Then he curled up and went to sleep. Around midnight he bumped into a bed of weeds. The tide is strong tonight, he thought. He rolled over in the water and slowly opened his eyes. There were strange things nosing about nearby!

Who in the Deep Sea are these? Kotick asked himself. They were like no creatures he had ever seen before. They were very long, with tails like shovels. Their heads were funny-looking. They stood on the ends of their tails in the deep water. And they waved their front flippers like arms.

"Good evening," said Kotick.

The big things bowed and waved their flippers some more. Then they went on eating. They tucked whole bushes of seaweed into their huge mouths.

"A messy way to eat," said Kotick.

The creatures bowed again, and Kotick got mad. "I can see you know how to bow," he said. "But I want to know your names."

The creatures' lips moved. Their glassy eyes stared. But the creatures said nothing.

"Well!" said Kotick. "You are the only animals I've met who are uglier than Sea Vitch. And who have worse manners."

Then he remembered what the gull had screamed to him years ago. He had found the Sea Cows at last!

The Sea Cows went on chewing and grazing in the weeds. Kotick asked them questions in every language he had learned. But the Sea Cows didn't answer because they couldn't talk.

At daylight the Sea Cows began to move slowly to the north. From time to time they stopped to bow to one another.

Kotick followed them. He said to himself, "These creatures are so stupid. They must have a safe island somewhere. Otherwise they would have been killed long ago. And any place good enough for them is good enough for seals. I just wish they would hurry."

But the Sea Cows went very, very slowly. Kotick swam around them. And over them. And under them. But he could not hurry them.

At last Kotick saw that the Sea Cows were following a warm current of water. He began to think that maybe they weren't so stupid.

One night the Sea Cows suddenly started to swim quickly. Kotick followed. He couldn't believe how fast they were moving.

The Sea Cows headed for a cliff by the shore. The cliff ran deep into the water. And far, far down at its bottom was a dark hole.

The Sea Cows swam into the hole. And Kotick followed. It was a long, long swim. He was gasping by the time they reached open water again.

"My goodness!" he said. "It was a long dive. But it was worth it." They were swimming along the edge of the nicest beach Kotick had ever seen. There were long stretches of smooth rock. Perfect places for raising baby seals, thought Kotick. There were playgrounds of hard sand. There were waves to dance in. There were sand dunes to climb on.

And best of all, Kotick could tell that no men had ever come to this place.

"It's like Northeast Point, but ten times better," he said. "The Sea Cows must be wiser than I thought. If any place in the sea is safe, this is it."

Paradise, at Last

Kotick was in a hurry to get back to Northeast Point. But it took him six days to go home. The first seal he saw once he arrived was the one who had been waiting for him. She looked into his eyes. At once she knew he had found his island.

But the other seals laughed at Kotick. One young seal said, "You can't order us off like this, Kotick. We've been fighting for our nesting spots. That's something you know nothing about. You spend all your time in the sea."

"I don't want to fight for a nesting spot," said Kotick. "I want to show you all a place where you will be safe."

"Are you trying to back away from a fight?" asked the young seal.

"Will you come with me if I fight and win?" asked Kotick.

"Very well," said the other young seal. "If you win, I'll come."

The young seal had no time to change his mind. Kotick roared and knocked him to the ground.

Then Kotick looked at the other seals. He said, "I've found an island where you'll be safe.

But you won't believe me. So I'm going to teach you something. Look out!"

Kotick threw himself at the biggest seal he saw. He bumped and banged that seal. Then he tossed him aside and charged at another. His eyes glowed like a flame. His teeth gleamed. He threw seals about as if they were fish.

Sea Catch gave a great roar. "Kotick may be a fool. But he's the best fighter on the beaches. I'm with you, my son!"

Then Sea Catch waddled in to join the fight. Matkah as well as the seal Kotick was going to marry sat back to watch.

It was a beautiful fight. And at last there were no seals left that dared to lift their heads. Kotick and his father went up and down the beach, roaring loudly.

That night Kotick climbed up on a bare rock. "I have taught you all a lesson," he said.

Sea Catch answered. "I am proud of you, son. And I will come with you to your island. If there is such a place."

"Hear that, fat pigs of the sea?" roared Kotick. "Who else will come with me?"

There was a sound like the ripple of the tide. "We will come," said thousands of voices. "We will follow Kotick, the white seal."

A week later Kotick led an army of seals to the Sea Cows' tunnel. Some seals stayed behind. They called Kotick and his followers foolish.

But the next spring these seals met Kotick's seals in the sea. They heard tales of the new beaches. So more and more seals left Northeast Point.

Of course, it did not all happen at once. Seals need to think about things for a long time. However, year after year, more seals leave. They go to Kotick's quiet beaches. The beaches where no man ever comes.

Mowgli's Brothers

ONE WARM NIGHT Father Wolf sat in his cave. Mother Wolf lay nearby with their four cubs.

Suddenly they heard a voice. "Good luck to you, Chief of the Wolves. And strong white teeth to your children."

It was the jackal, Tabaqui. He was always looking for food.

"Enter," said Father Wolf. "But there is no food here."

"Not for a wolf," said Tabaqui as he came into the cave. "Though I will be happy with this bone."

Tabaqui chewed before saying, "Shere Khan, the tiger, has new hunting grounds. He will hunt in these hills," he said.

"He has no right!" cried Father Wolf. "By the Law of the Jungle, he should not come here. He will scare off all the game."

Mother Wolf added, "He will make the villagers angry. They will come after him. And they will set the grass on fire."

"I hear him now," said Tabaqui. "Should I tell him you do not want him here?"

"Out!" snapped Father Wolf.

Tabaqui left, and Father Wolf listened. He heard the dry, snarly call of a tiger who has caught nothing.

"The fool!" said Father Wolf. "To make such noise! Does he think our deer are fat cattle waiting to be caught?"

"It is not deer he hunts tonight," said Mother Wolf. "It is Man."

"Man!" cried Father Wolf. "Why can't he hunt beetles and frogs?"

A Man-Cub Arrives at the Doorstep

There was a noise in the bushes. "Something is coming," said Mother Wolf.

Father Wolf got ready to leap. But he

stopped when he saw a naked baby in front of him.

"A man's cub!" Father Wolf cried. "Look!"

"A man's cub?" said Mother Wolf. "I have never seen one before. Bring it here."

Father Wolf gently picked up the man-cub. He put it down next to Mother Wolf.

"How little!" she said. "And how brave!"

"I could kill him with a touch of my paw," said Father Wolf. "Yet he is not afraid."

Then something blocked the light. It was the tiger, Shere Khan. Only his head could fit into the opening of the cave.

"You honor us, Shere Khan," said Father Wolf. But his eyes showed how angry he was. "What do you want?"

"The man-cub I was hunting. I followed it here after its parents ran off," the tiger said.

"The man-cub is ours," said Father Wolf. "To kill if we want."

The tiger's angry roar filled the cave. Mother Wolf jumped forward, her eyes glowing like two green moons.

"The man's cub is mine!" she cried. "He will live to hunt with the Pack. And one day he will hunt you! Now go!"

Shere knew Mother Wolf would fight to the death. So he pulled his head out of the cave.

"We will see what the Pack has to say about this!" the tiger shouted. He ran off crying, "The cub is mine! My teeth will have him in the end!"

Father Wolf turned to Mother Wolf. He asked, "Are you sure you want to keep him?"

"He came to us alone and hungry," she said. "Yet he was not afraid. That tiger would have killed him! And then the villagers would have killed us! So, yes, I will keep him."

She turned to the man-cub. "Lie still, little frog. That is what I will call you. 'Mowgli the Frog.' And one day you will hunt Shere Khan. Just as he hunted you," she said.

Then Father Wolf said, "But the tiger spoke the truth. We must show the man-cub to the Pack."

The Law of the Jungle says that every wolf must show his cubs to the Pack Council. This is so all the Pack knows its cubs.

The Pack Council Rules

Soon it was time for the Council to meet. Father and Mother Wolf took their cubs to the Council Rock. They also took Mowgli, the man-cub.

Akela, the leader of the Pack, lay on top of

the rock. Below him, 40 or more wolves sat in a circle. Cubs rolled around in the center of the circle. Now and then a wolf looked a cub over carefully. Now and then a mother or father pushed a cub forward. They didn't want their cubs to be missed.

Akela cried out, "You know the Law. Look well, O Wolves. Look at these cubs who are part of our Pack."

At last Father Wolf pushed Mowgli into the center. The man-cub sat there and laughed.

Again Akela said, "Look well, O Wolves."

A roar came from behind the rocks. It was Shere Khan. "The man-cub is mine. Give him to me. What do the Wolves want with a man's cub?"

Akela just said, "Who should the Wolves listen to? Only the Wolves."

But a young wolf repeated Shere Khan's question. "What do the Wolves want with a man's cub?" he said.

Now the Law of the Jungle is clear. Anyone can question the right of a cub to be part of the Pack. If this happens, the cub must be spoken for by two members of the Pack. Two members who are not the cub's parents.

"Who speaks for this cub?" asked Akela. For a long time there was no answer.

At last someone spoke up. It was Baloo, the sleepy brown bear. Baloo was the only other animal allowed at the Council. For it was Baloo who taught the cubs the Law of the Jungle.

"I speak for the man's cub," said Baloo. "There is no harm in him. Let him run with the Pack."

"We need another," said Akela. "Who else will speak for the man-cub?"

A black shadow dropped down into the circle. It was Bagheera, the panther. Bagheera was both clever and bold. His voice was like wild honey dripping from a tree.

"I have no right to speak here," Bagheera purred. "But the Law of the Jungle says that a cub may be bought at a price. Am I right?"

"Yes!" cried the young wolves. "The cub can be bought. It is the Law."

Then Bagheera said, "To kill a naked cub is wrong. Let him grow. Then killing him will be more sport for you. Baloo has spoken for the cub. Now I will pay one newly killed bull for him. The bull is yours if you let the man-cub be part of your Pack."

The Wolves said, "What does it matter? The cub will die in the winter rains. Or in the summer sun. Let him run with the Pack."

So Akela cried out again. "Look well, O Wolves!"

One by one, the wolves came to look at Mowgli. Then they went off to get the bull Bagheera had killed.

Only Akela, Baloo, Bagheera, and Mowgli's own wolves stayed behind. "Men and their cubs are very wise," said Akela. "This one may be a help to us someday. So take him away. Train him as he should be trained."

And that is how Mowgli became a member of the Wolf Pack.

Mowgli Grows Up

You must guess at what happened for the next 10 or 11 years. Because if it were all written, it would fill many books. You only need to know that Mowgli led a wonderful life with the Wolves.

Father Wolf taught him the ways of the jungle. Soon Mowgli understood every rustle in the grass. Every breath of the night air. Every note of the owls. Every splash of every little fish.

When he was not learning, Mowgli sat in the sun. He slept, ate, and went to sleep again. He swam in the forest pools.

Mowgli took his place at the Council Rock too. There he learned something. If he stared hard at a wolf, the wolf dropped his eyes. And so Mowgli stared just for fun. But he also helped his Wolf Brothers. He would pick thorns from the tender pads of their feet. They could not do this themselves.

As the years passed, Mowgli came across Shere Khan more often. For Akela was growing weaker and weaker. At the same time Shere Khan was making friends with the younger wolves. Akela wouldn't have let this happen if he had been stronger.

Shere Khan told the young wolves what fine hunters they were. He asked if they wanted to be led by a dying wolf. He said, "I hear that you can't look the man-cub in the eyes." At his words, the young wolves growled and grew angry.

Bagheera knew something of this. He told Mowgli that Shere Khan would kill him someday.

But Mowgli laughed. "I have the Pack. I have you and Baloo. Why should I be afraid?"

One warm day Bagheera spoke of the tiger again. "Little Brother," he said. "How often have I told you that Shere Khan is your enemy?"

"As many times as there are nuts on that

palm tree," said Mowgli. "What of it? Shere Khan is all long tail and loud talk."

"Open your eyes, Little Brother," warned Bagheera. "Shere Khan doesn't dare kill you now. But Akela is very old. Soon the day will come when he misses his kill. Then he will lead the Pack no more. Shere Khan has talked to the young wolves. He has told them that a man-cub has no place in the Pack. And they believe him."

"I was born in the jungle," said Mowgli. "I have obeyed the Law. I have pulled thorns from the paws of every wolf in our Pack. They are my brothers!"

"You are a man's cub," said Bagheera in his soft voice. "*Men* are your brothers. And you must go back to them someday. If you are not killed by the young wolves first."

"Why would they want to kill me?" asked Mowgli.

"Look at me," said Bagheera. And Mowgli stared at him. After half a minute the panther turned his eyes away.

"That is why," he said. "Even I cannot look you in the eyes. And I love you, Little Brother. The others hate you because they cannot meet your eyes. And because you are wise. But they hate you most of all for being a man."

"I did not know these things," said Mowgli.

"What is the Law of the Jungle?" said Bagheera. "Strike first. And that is what you must be ready to do. I am sure that Akela will miss his next kill. The Pack will turn against him. And against you. They will have a meeting at the Council Rock. And then—"

Bagheera went on. "You must go to the village below. Take some of the Red Flower they grow there. Then when the time comes, you will have a strong friend. Even stronger than those of us who love you."

By the Red Flower, Bagheera meant fire. No creature in the jungle will call fire by its name. Every creature lives in deadly fear of it.

"The Red Flower?" said Mowgli. "It grows outside their huts at night. I will get some."

"Remember that it grows in little pots," said Bagheera. "Get one quickly. Then keep it with you until you need it."

So that night Mowgli headed down the hill. He stopped when he heard the sound of the Pack hunting. He heard the snap of teeth and then a yelp. He heard the young wolves shouting Akela's name. And he knew that Akela had missed his kill.

Mowgli ran on to the village. There he watched through the windows all night long.

In the morning he saw a child pick up a pot of red-hot coals. When the child carried the pot outside, Mowgli took it. Then he disappeared into the jungle.

As he walked, Mowgli fed the fire twigs and dried bark. Halfway up the hill, he met Bagheera.

"Akela has missed his deer," the panther said. "The younger wolves would have killed him last night. But they wanted you too."

"I am ready," said Mowgli.

Mowgli Leaves the Jungle

Later that day he set off for the Council Rock. Akela lay by the side of the rock, not on top of it. Shere Khan and his young wolves stood nearby.

Mowgli sat down with Bagheera at his side. The fire pot was between them.

Shere Khan began to speak. Bagheera whispered to Mowgli. "He has no right to speak here. Say so!"

Mowgli jumped to his feet. "O Wolves!" he cried. "What does a tiger have to do with us?"

There was much grumbling and shouting. But at last some of the older wolves cried, "Mowgli is right. Let Akela speak!"

Akela lifted his tired old head. "For 12 seasons I have led you. Now I have missed my kill. So now you have the right to kill me. But I have the right to fight you, one by one."

There was a long silence. For no one wanted to fight Akela to the death.

Shere Khan roared. "Do not listen to this toothless fool! He will be dead soon. And the man-cub should be too. He was my meat from the first. Give him to me."

Many in the Pack yelled, "Give the man to Shere Khan!"

But Akela spoke again. "Mowgli has eaten our food. He has slept with us. He has helped us hunt. He has obeyed the Law of the Jungle."

"He is a man!" shouted Shere Khan. "No man should run with the creatures of the jungle. Give him to me!"

"He is our brother in all but blood," said Akela. "Yet you would kill him! I have lived too long to see such a day."

Akela went on. "I will tell you this. If you let Mowgli go unharmed, I will die without fighting. That will save the Pack many lives. And it will keep you from killing a brother."

"He is a man!" shouted some of the Wolves.

"There is nothing more to be done," Bagheera whispered to Mowgli. "We must fight."

Mowgli stood up with the fire pot in his hands. "Listen!" he cried. "You say I am a man. And I feel your words are true. So I will not call you my brothers anymore. I will call you dogs, as a man should. And I have something here that you dogs fear. I have some of the Red Flower."

He threw the pot onto the ground. The hot coals lit the dry grass. The Wolves drew back in fear.

Then Mowgli stuck a dead branch into the fire. When it caught fire, he swung it over his head.

"Save Akela," whispered Bagheera. "He has always been your friend."

Mowgli shouted, "I see that you are all dogs! So I will forget that I am your brother. But I promise that I will not betray you. There will be no war between me and the Pack."

Then Mowgli spun around to face Shere Khan. "But there is war between us, jungle cat. Stir a whisker, and I will ram the Red Flower down your throat!" He beat the tiger over the head with the burning branch. "Now go from here!"

Shere Khan ran off. Then Mowgli turned back to the Pack. "Akela will live as he pleases. You will not kill him because I tell you not to. Now go. All of you!"

Mowgli struck right and left with the burning branch. The Wolves ran off with sparks burning their fur.

Soon only Akela, Bagheera, and about ten wolves who loved Mowgli were left.

Tears ran down Mowgli's face. "What is this?" he said. "Am I dying?"

"No, Little Brother," said Bagheera. "Those are only tears. Now I know you are a man. Let the tears fall, Mowgli."

So Mowgli cried as if his heart would break. He had never cried in his life before.

When he was done crying, Mowgli said, "I will go to men. But I must say good-bye to my mother." And he went to the cave and cried on her coat. The cubs howled along with him.

"You will not forget me?" he asked.

"Never!" promised the cubs. "When you are a man, come to the foot of the hill. We will visit you there."

"Come soon!" cried Father Wolf.

"Come soon," whispered Mother Wolf. "For I loved you more than I loved my own cubs."

"I will come," said Mowgli. "And when I do, I will bring Shere Khan's hide with me. I will lay it out on the Council Rock. Tell them in the jungle not to forget me!"

Day was just coming when Mowgli left. He went down the hillside alone. To meet those strange creatures called *men*.

THE PLAY

Cast of Characters

Storyteller
Mowgli
Priest*
Man of the village*
Head Man of the village*
Messua
Buldeo, the village hunter
Gray Brother, the eldest wolf cub
Akela, former leader of the Pack
Shere Khan, the tiger
Mother Wolf*

Setting: A village on the outskirts of the jungle

* Since these roles are small, one student could read several parts.

Act One

Storyteller: After Mowgli left the Wolf Pack, he walked to a valley some 20 miles away. He walked until he came to a village gate. Mowgli had seen such gates before. He knew they were to keep wild animals out of the village.

Mowgli: So the men here are afraid of the creatures of the jungle.

Priest: Who is this?

Man: He looks like a wild boy.

Storyteller: Mowgli couldn't understand the villagers. He only knew the languages of the jungle creatures. And the villagers couldn't understand him. For he spoke in the words of the wolves.

Mowgli: They have no manners, these men. They chatter like the gray ape.

Priest: He is nothing to be afraid of. He is just a wolf-child who has run away from the jungle. See—his arms and legs are covered with bites.

Man: You are right. And he is a handsome boy too. In fact, Messua, he is like your son. Your son who was taken by the tiger long ago.

Messua: Let me look. No, this boy is thinner. But he has the look of my boy.

Priest: What the jungle has taken, the jungle has given back. Take the boy to your house, Messua.

Mowgli: All this talking! It's like the new cubs being looked over by the Pack.

Messua: Come this way, boy.

Storyteller: So Messua took Mowgli to her hut. There she gave him some milk and bread. Then she looked into his eyes.

Messua: I thought that maybe you were my son, Nathoo. Come back to me from the jungle. But I see that you do not know that name. Still, you are very like my Nathoo. So you shall be my son.

Mowgli: I am not sure I want to stay here. I don't like having a roof over my head.

Messua: I don't know what you are saying, my son.

Mowgli: What good is it if I can't understand a man's words? I must learn to speak their language.

Storyteller: Now Mowgli had learned many languages in the jungle. So it was easy for him to learn to speak like a man. As soon as Messua said a word, Mowgli would say it back. Before dark he had learned the names of many things in the hut. But at bedtime Mowgli wouldn't sleep inside. When Messua shut the door of the hut, Mowgli went out the window. He found a spot in the long grass at the edge of the field. Before he could close his eyes, a soft nose poked him.

Gray Brother: Phew! You smell of smoke and cows. Like a man already. Wake up, Little Brother. I bring news.

Mowgli: I am glad to see you! Is everyone in the jungle all right?

Gray Brother: Everyone except for the wolves you burned. Now listen to me. Shere Khan, the tiger, has gone off to hunt. And to let his coat grow in again. For you burned him badly. But he will be back. And he said he will bury your bones.

Mowgli: There are two sides to that story. Still, news is always good. Say that you will bring me your news again.

Gray Brother: You won't forget that you are a wolf? You won't let the men make you forget?

Mowgli: Never. I will always remember that I love you. And all the wolves in our cave. But I will remember something else. That I was thrown out of the Pack.

Gray Brother: You may be thrown out of another pack as well. Men are only men, Little Brother. Their talk is like that of frogs in the pond. I will come again. I will wait for you at the far edge of the field.

Act Two

Storyteller: For the next three months, Mowgli stayed close to the village. He learned about clothing, money, and farming. Mowgli didn't see the sense of any of these things. Still, he did as men did.

But there was one thing that Mowgli couldn't seem to learn. That was the difference that caste makes between men. For in India, men belong to different groups, or castes. Those in higher castes have nothing to do with those in lower ones. This Mowgli could not understand.

One day Mowgli stopped to help the village potter. And the potter was a low-caste man.

Priest: Messua, you must set your son to work at once. So he will not be doing such foolish things. Helping the potter! What will he do next?

Head Man: Yes. He must go out with the buffalo tomorrow. He must watch them in the fields.

Storyteller: Since Mowgli was now a worker, he went to the village club that night. This was a spot where the people met to talk. When Mowgli arrived, Buldeo the hunter was telling one of his stories.

Buldeo: Ah, my friends. The beasts of the jungle are to be feared. The deer and the wild pig dig up our crops. And a tiger carried off a man the other night. Right in sight of the village gates! But this tiger is a ghost! The ghost of the wicked old moneylender who died years ago.

Man: Are you sure?

Buldeo: My story is true. The tiger is a ghost. You see, the moneylender limped. And so does this tiger. You can tell from his tracks.

Man: Then this must be the truth.

Mowgli: It is not true! These tales are cobwebs and moon talk! The tiger is called Shere Khan. And he limps because he was born with a bad leg. Everyone in the jungle knows that.

Buldeo: Ah! So the jungle brat has something to say! If you are so smart, bring the tiger's skin to the village.

Mowgli: I have been listening all evening. And you have not said one true thing.

Head Man: It is time for this boy to go herding.

Mowgli: I will go. Tomorrow.

Act Three

Storyteller: The next morning Mowgli sat on the back of Rama, the great bull. The buffalo followed them to the edge of the plain. There Mowgli dropped from Rama's back. He ran off to the edge of the jungle, where Gray Brother waited.

Gray Brother: I have been here for days. What is the meaning of this? Are you a cattle herder now?

Mowgli: I must be a herder for a while. Do you have any news of Shere Khan?

Gray Brother: He has come back. He waited a long time, hoping to find you. Now he has gone off again to find some game. But he still means to kill you.

Mowgli: Very good. As long as he is gone, you must sit on this rock here. Then I can see you when I leave the village. If the tiger comes back, wait for me by the tree in the center of the plain. That way I will know he is back.

Gray Brother: I will do it.

Mowgli: Good-bye, my brother. Now I will rest while the buffalo eat grass. For herding is a lazy job.

Storyteller: Day after day Mowgli led the buffalo out of the village. And day after day he saw Gray Brother sitting on the rock. So he knew that Shere Khan had not come back. Until—

Mowgli: Oh! Gray Brother is not in his usual place. I must go and meet him at the tree.

Gray Brother: There you are! Shere Khan came back last night. He and Tabaqui, the jackal.

Mowgli: I am not afraid of Shere Khan. But Tabaqui is very smart.

Gray Brother: Have no fear. I have talked to Tabaqui. He told me everything before I broke his back.

Mowgli: What did he say?

Gray Brother: Shere Khan has a plan. Tonight he will come for you.

Mowgli: Has he eaten today? Or does he hunt on an empty stomach?

Gray Brother: He killed at dawn. A pig. So his belly is full. Now he is sleeping.

Mowgli: The fool! And he thinks that I will wait until he is rested! Where is he? We can take care of him as he sleeps. If only I could speak the buffalo's language. I would tell them to charge at the tiger. But maybe we can fix it so they smell him. Can we get behind him so the wind carries his smell to the buffalo?

Gray Brother: No. Shere Khan swam in the river. So they will not smell him.

Mowgli: Tabaqui must have told him to do that. He would never have thought of it on his own. I could take the herd to the far end of the river valley. But then Shere Khan would sneak out the other end. If only I had two herds of buffalo. Gray Brother, can you split the herd in two for me?

Gray Brother: Not by myself. But I have brought a helper.

Akela: Greetings, Brother.

Mowgli: Akela! Akela! I should have known you wouldn't forget me.

Gray Brother: Tell us what we must do.

Mowgli: We must cut the herd in two. You keep the cows and calves together. Akela and I will take the bulls.

Storyteller: The two wolves ran in and out of the herd. Soon the buffalo were in two groups. The cows made a circle around the calves. The bulls stood by themselves, snorting and stamping.

Akela: Watch them! Don't let them get back together again!

Mowgli: You drive the bulls to the left, Akela. I will come with you.

Gray Brother: What shall I do?

Mowgli: You drive the cows and calves to the other end of the valley.

Gray Brother: How far should I go?

Mowgli: To a place where the sides of the valley are high. Too high for Shere Khan to climb. Keep the cows and calves there until we come!

Akela: And I will drive the bulls the other way.

Mowgli: They are moving! Careful, careful, Akela! Did you think these creatures could move so fast?

Akela: I have hunted buffalo in my day, Little Brother. Now, shall I turn them into the jungle?

Mowgli: Yes. We will make a big circle. We will be at one end of the valley with the bulls. Gray Brother will be at the other end with the cows and calves. Shere Khan will be caught in the middle.

Storyteller: Mowgli and Akela drove the bulls to the edge of the valley. They stopped and looked down. The hills were very steep. Too steep for Shere Khan to climb.

Mowgli: Now we have Shere Khan in our trap. Shere Khan! Shere Khan! Wake up, tiger!

Shere Khan: Who calls?

Mowgli: It is I! Mowgli!

Akela: Do we move now?

Mowgli: Yes! Hurry the bulls down the hillside!

Storyteller: The herd went downhill like a river of horns and hooves. Once they started, there was no stopping them. Shere Khan heard them coming. He headed the other way. But the sides of the valley were steep. He had to keep going along the river. The bulls came along behind him. And then Shere Khan met up with the cows and calves. They were coming from the other end of the valley. The tiger was caught in a storm of stamping, snorting buffalo.

Mowgli: Quick, Akela! It is over now! Break up the herd! Or they will start fighting with one another.

Akela: It is truly over. The tiger is dead. He is trampled into the ground.

Mowgli: That was a dog's death. But his hide will look fine on the Council Rock. I will skin him.

Gray Brother: Listen! Someone is coming!

Buldeo: We heard the buffalo all the way back in the village. Don't you know how to take care of them? And what are you doing now? Skinning a tiger? Why, that is the tiger that limps! Get away from here, boy! There is a reward for the tiger! And I will collect it! Not you!

Mowgli: Akela, this man is bothering me. Take care of him!

Akela: Happily, Little Brother.

Buldeo: No! No! Get the wolf off me! He will kill me!

Mowgli: He will not kill you, Buldeo. And I will not let you collect the reward. There is an old war between this tiger and myself. A very old war. And I have won!

Buldeo: I am lost! This is magic! Will you turn into a tiger too, boy?

Mowgli: Yes.

Buldeo: I didn't know you were more than a herd boy. Let me go. Don't let your servant the wolf tear me to pieces.

Mowgli: Go in peace, then. And next time, don't try to take my kill. Akela, let him get up.

Storyteller: So Akela backed away. Buldeo ran back to the village as fast as he could. There he told stories of magic. Stories that made the priest frown. Meanwhile, Mowgli went on with his work. It was almost dark by the time he had skinned the tiger.

Mowgli: Help me, Akela. We must herd the buffalo back to the village now.

Storyteller: When they got near the village, Mowgli saw lights. Half the village seemed to be waiting at the gates.

Mowgli: They are waiting to thank me for killing the tiger.

Akela: Don't be so sure about that, Little Brother.

Buldeo: Wolf's brat! Here is a shower of stones for you!

Head Man: Jungle devil! Go away from here!

Priest: Go quickly, or I will turn you into a wolf again!

Head Man: Shoot, Buldeo! Shoot!

Mowgli: What is this?

Akela: They are like the Pack. They are throwing you out of their village.

Priest: Wolf! Wolf's cub! Go away!

Mowgli: Again? Last time it was because I was a man. This time it is because I am a wolf. Let's go, Akela.

Akela: Wait, Mowgli! This woman is running to you.

Messua: Oh, my son, my son. They say you can change yourself into a wolf. I do not believe that. But you must go. If you don't, they will kill you.

Mowgli: It is just another of their silly

stories. Now run back quickly. For I am going to send the herd into the village.

Akela: Now, Mowgli?

Mowgli: Yes! Bring the herd in, Akela!

Storyteller: The buffalo hardly needed to be herded. They charged through the village gate. The crowd ran left and right.

Mowgli: Count your buffalo! After all, I may have stolen one! And you can thank Messua that I do not come after you with my wolves! Because she was kind to me.

Akela: Mowgli, we must leave.

Storyteller: Soon the moon rose over the plain. The villagers could see Mowgli and the two wolves walking into the jungle. The men banged on their bells and made noise. And Buldeo began telling stories about his adventures. The moon was just going down when Mowgli and the wolves reached the Council Rock. Mother Wolf was waiting there with the other wolves.

Mowgli: They have thrown me out of the Man-Pack, Mother Wolf. But I have kept my word. I have brought Shere Khan's hide to you.

Mother Wolf: I told the tiger. I told him that one day the hunter would be the hunted.

Mowgli: Look well, O Wolves. Look at the hide of Shere Khan! Have I kept my word?

Akela: Yes!

Mother Wolf: Yes!

Gray Brother: Will you stay with us now, Mowgli?

Mowgli: The Man-Pack threw me out. The Wolf-Pack threw me out. Now I will hunt alone in the jungle.

Gray Brother: Then I will come with you. And so will my three brothers.

Storyteller: So Mowgli went away. He hunted in the jungle with his four brothers, the wolf cubs. But he was not alone forever. Years afterward he married. But that is a story for later.